THE JUNGLE Book

A GOLDEN BOOK • NEW YORK

randomhouse.com/kids
ISBN 978-0-7364-2096-9
Printed in the United States of America
40 39 38 37 36 35

Many strange legends are told of the jungles
of far-off India. They speak of Bagheera the black
panther, and of Baloo the bear. They tell of Kaa
the sly python, and of the lord of the jungle, the great
tiger Shere Khan. But of all these legends, none is so
strange as the story of a small boy named Mowgli.

A child, left all alone in the jungle, was found by Bagheera the panther. Bagheera could not give the small, helpless Man-cub care and nourishment, so he took the boy to the den of a wolf family with young cubs of their own.

That is how it happened that Mowgli, as the Man-cub came to be called, was raised among the wolves.

Mowgli had lived with the wolves for ten years when the wolf pack called a meeting at Council Rock. "As you know," said Akela, the leader of the pack, "Shere Khan the tiger has returned. If he learns that our pack is harboring a Man-cub, danger will be doubled for all our families. The Man-cub can no longer stay with the pack."

Out of the shadows stepped Bagheera
the panther. "Perhaps I can be of help," said
Bagheera. "I know of a Man-village where
he'll be safe."

So it was arranged, and when the greenish light of the jungle morning slipped through the leaves, Bagheera and Mowgli set out.

All day they walked, and when night fell, they slept on a high branch of a giant banyan tree. All this seemed like an adventure to Mowgli. But when he learned that he was to leave the jungle, he was horrified.

"No!" cried Mowgli. "I want to stay in the
jungle. I'm not afraid. I can look out for myself."
   He slipped down a length of trailing vine and
ran away.

Mowgli soon met a bumbling bear named Baloo. Baloo played games with Mowgli and taught him to live a life of ease. There were coconuts to crack, bananas to peel, and sweet, juicy pawpaws to pick from jungle trees.

Colonel Hathi, the proud old leader
of the elephant herd, tried to train young
Mowgli in military drills as he led his
troop, trumpeting down the jungle trails.
   Mowgli was having such fun in
the jungle!

But the jungle *was* dangerous.

Sly old Kaa the python would have loved to squeeze Mowgli tight in his coils.

But Shere Khan the tiger was the real danger to Mowgli. That was because Shere Khan, like all tigers, had a hatred of man.

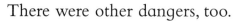

There were other dangers, too.

One day, Baloo and Mowgli were enjoying
a dip in a jungle river. Suddenly, down swooped the
monkey folk. They snatched Mowgli from the
water before Baloo knew what was happening.

They tossed him through the air from hand to
hand and swung away with him through the trees.

Off in the jungle, Bagheera heard Mowgli's cry and came with a leap and a bound.

"The monkeys have carried him off!" gasped Baloo.

Bagheera and Baloo raced to the ruined city where the monkeys made their home. They found Mowgli a prisoner of the monkey king.

"Teach me the secret of man's red fire," the monkey king ordered Mowgli, "so I can be like you."

It took quite a fight for Bagheera and Baloo to rescue Mowgli!

"Look, Mowgli," said Baloo. "I gotta take you to the Man-village."

But alas, the boy would not listen. He kicked up his heels and ran away again.

This time, his wanderings led him to the high grass, where Shere Khan lay waiting, smiling a hungry smile.

When Mowgli caught sight of the tiger, Shere Khan asked, "Well, Man-cub, aren't you going to run?"

But Mowgli did not have the wisdom to be afraid. "Why should I run?" he asked, staring at Shere Khan as the tiger gathered himself to pounce. "You don't scare me."

"That foolish boy!" growled Bagheera,
who had crept close just in time to hear Mowgli.
Both Bagheera and Baloo flung themselves
upon the lord of the jungle, to save Mowgli
once more.

They were brave and strong, but the tiger was mighty of tooth and claw.

There was a flash of lightning, and a dead tree nearby caught fire. Mowgli snatched a burning branch and tied it to Shere Khan's tail. The tiger, terrified, ran away. Mowgli was very pleased with himself as he strutted between the two weary warriors, Bagheera and Baloo.

A little later, Mowgli reached the Man-village. From ahead came a sound he did not know. He peeked through a bush. It was the song of a village girl who had come to fill her water jug.

As he listened to the soft notes of her song, Mowgli felt that he must follow the girl. He crept up the path to the village, drawn by the girl and her song.

Baloo and Bagheera watched the boy's small figure as long as it could be seen. When Mowgli vanished inside the village gate, Bagheera sighed a deep sigh.

"It was bound to happen," he said. "Mowgli is where he belongs now."